910   Sandak, Cass
San   Remote places

DATE DUE

MAR 3 1 '92			

MONTEREY PENINSULA
UNIFIED SCHOOL DISTRICT
MONTEREY, CALIFORNIA

DEMCO

NEW FRONTIERS
EXPLORATION IN THE 20th CENTURY

REMOTE PLACES

CASS R. SANDAK

FRANKLIN WATTS
NEW YORK LONDON TORONTO SYDNEY

Photographs courtesy of: Annie Griffiths/Bruce Coleman, Inc.: title page; Norman Benton/Peter Arnold, Inc.: p.4; Klaus Payson/Peter Arnold, Inc.: p.5 (top left); Stephen Dalton/NHPA: p.5 (top right); Martin Johnson/American Museum of Natural History: p. 5 (bottom); Tom McHugh/Photo Researchers: p. 7 (top); Victor Englebert p. 7 (bottom left), p. 9 (top), p. 14; Toby Bankett Pyle/Photo Researchers: p. 7 (bottom right); UPI/Bettman Newsphotos: p. 8 (bottom center); Jacques Jangoux/Peter Arnold, Inc.: p. 8 (left), p. 9 (bottom), p. 11 (bottom), p. 13 (top left); Herbert Lang/American Museum of Natural History: p. 10 (top right); The Granger Collection, New York: p. 10 (bottom left); Baron Hugo van Lawick/National Geographic Society: p. 11 (top); Daily Telegraph: p. 11 (center); Yoram Lehman/Peter Arnold, Inc.: p. 12 (bottom left); Jen and Des Bartlett/Bruce Coleman, Inc.: p. 12 (bottom right); Georg Gerster/Photo Researchers: p. 13 (top right), p. 29 (top left); Klaus D. Francke/Peter Arnold, Inc.: p. 13 (bottom); Ted Hutchinson/A.N.T./NHPA: p. 15 (top left); American Museum of Natural History: p. 15 (top right); Photo Researchers: p. 15 (bottom); Bruno J. Zehnder/Peter Arnold, Inc.: p. 16 (left); Shackelford/American Museum of Natural History: p. 16 (right); Gianni T./Photo Researchers, Inc.: p. 17 (top left); American Museum of Natural History: p. 17 (top right); Helmut Gritscher/Peter Arnold, Inc.: p. 19 (top); Vittoriano Rastelli/Time Magazine: p. 19 (center); Paolo Koch/Photo Researchers: p. 19 (bottom); John Roshilley/Photo Researchers: p. 21 (top right); Bill O' Connor/Peter Arnold, Inc.: p. 21 (bottom); Warming/Gaworski/Taurus Photos, N.Y.C.: p. 22 (bottom); Michael Giannechini/Photo Researchers: p. 23 (left); Kevin B. Gale/Taurus Photos, N.Y.C.: p. 23 (right); Walter H. Hodge/Peter Arnold, Inc.: p. 24 (right); Michael Friedel/Woodfin Camp & Associates: p. 24 (bottom); Ragnar Larusson/Photo Researchers: p. 25 (top); Fred Bavendam/Peter Arnold, Inc.: p. 25 (bottom); Bob Evans/Peter Arnold, Inc.: p. 26 (top); Ronald F. Thomas/Taurus Photos, N.Y.C.: p. 26 (bottom); Francis LeGuen/Photo Researchers: p. 27 (top), p. 27 (bottom); AP/Wide World Photos: p. 27 (center); NASA: p. 28; Luiz Claudio Marigo/Peter Arnold, Inc. p. 29 (top right); Thomas Hopker/Woodfin Camp & Associates: p. 29 (bottom).

FOR MY MOTHER

First published in the USA
by Franklin Watts Inc.
387 Park Ave. South
New York, N.Y. 10016

First published in 1989 by
Franklin Watts
12a Golden Square
London W1R 4BA

First published in Australia
by Franklin Watts
Australia
14 Mars Road
Lane Cove, NSW 2066

US ISBN: 0-531-10458-3
UK ISBN: 0 86313 530 7
Library of Congress
Catalog Card No: 87-50905

Designed by Michael Cooper

TABLE OF CONTENTS

THE KEY TO DISCOVERY

As the twentieth century draws to a close, there are few unvisited or unknown spots left. Despite tremendous technological advances, there are still, however, some places that remain relatively untouched. The peaks of mountains, the dense interiors of hidden rainforests and the parched stretches of the world's deserts are among the last outposts to be discovered, mapped and charted by the world's explorers.

Today's explorers are likely to be scientists: They are men and women looking for answers as much as they are seeking adventure. As they search for personal fulfillment, today's discoverers gain information and knowledge that will benefit all of humanity. What compels these men and women to risk their lives and limbs in the search for unknown regions? Curiosity is the key to exploration.

The push to explore and describe Earth's last unknown regions began in the nineteenth century. That period saw the birth of both Britain's Royal Geographical Society and America's National Geographic Society. They sponsored expeditions, journals, popular books and other publications devoted to geographic knowledge. The public eagerly awaited news of the latest exploits of popular heroes who explored Africa, South America and the remoter portions of Asia. Death in the field transformed some explorers into martyrs of science.

The twentieth century has witnessed air travel and improved land travel, shrinking the time it takes to reach even the most distant places. World War II generated many advances in technology that enabled explorers to expand the range of modern discovery.

The development of photography has made the farthest points of the globe accessible, even to armchair explorers. Daily news reports and documentaries detail the experiences of men and women exploring Earth's remote places. Photographs and TV cameras bring the depths of caves or the peaks of the highest mountains into our own homes. In 1988 a Japanese team became the first mountain climbers to send live video film, via satellite, of their conquest of Mount Everest.

One of the world's most remote places: the golden peak of Annapurna, one of the tallest of the Himalayas. The mountain's top was not reached until 1950, when a French team headed by Maurice Herzog scaled the summit.

Remote may mean distant from the centers of modern civilization
but not necessarily primitive. The unique peoples who live in Earth's
remote places are heirs to ancient cultures with highly developed
social networks. But as habitats disappear, so do the lifeforms and
cultures that these habitats support. Frequently the scientist/explorer
is called on to document a vanishing way of life—for example, the
Yahgan Indians of Tierra del Fuego or the much-changed Bedouins.
Were it not for the work of anthropologists, archaeologists,
botanists, linguists, zoologists and entomologists, a priceless
heritage would be lost. Often it takes an explorer with a pioneering
spirit to see from a totally new perspective something that is
already known.

Sometimes researchers in the field come face-to-face with
danger. The remote corners of the world are the last strongholds
of Earth's wildest and most powerful creatures, the largest reptiles
and the most deadly insects. One of the keys to successful
exploration is adaptability, as when the American explorers Martin
and Osa Johnson attended a cannibal feast but coolly declined to
partake of the main dish (which could have been themselves!).

The American
explorer/adventurer/writer
Osa Johnson in a photo
taken by her husband,
Martin, in their house in
Africa.

RAINFORESTS

The first rainforests that Europeans came to know were those of Asia. In fact, the term "jungle" comes from the Hindustani word *jangal*. It is an Anglo-Indian word for a dense forest or tangled wilderness. Rainforests cover only about 7 percent of the Earth's surface, but scientists estimate that approximately half of the world's species of plants and animals live in these rainforests. What they all have in common is lush vegetation brought about by heavy rainfall, often up to 250 cm (100 in) or more per year.

Some of the features of the rainforest are thick vines, snaking roots, immense trees and dense underbrush. Living in this lush backdrop are giant spiders, disease-carrying mosquitoes, deadly snakes and armies of ants. The soil is alive with worms, grubs and insects.

Exploration of the rainforests calls for a combination of skills. Sometimes great rivers and their tributaries are the only "roads" through the rainforests. Explorers must take their boats or rafts through churning rapids and avoid the rocks that lie as hazards in the rivers. Often it is necessary to hack a trail through the thick undergrowth with a machete.

There are stretches of rainforest on the great islands and peninsula off the coast of Southeast Asia—Sumatra, New Guinea and Malaya. The jungles of Borneo are among the world's most dangerous. Among the residents are ants that are 5 cm (2 in) long and carnivorous (meat-eating) plants that usually restrict their diets

The green areas show the world's largest concentrations of rainforests.

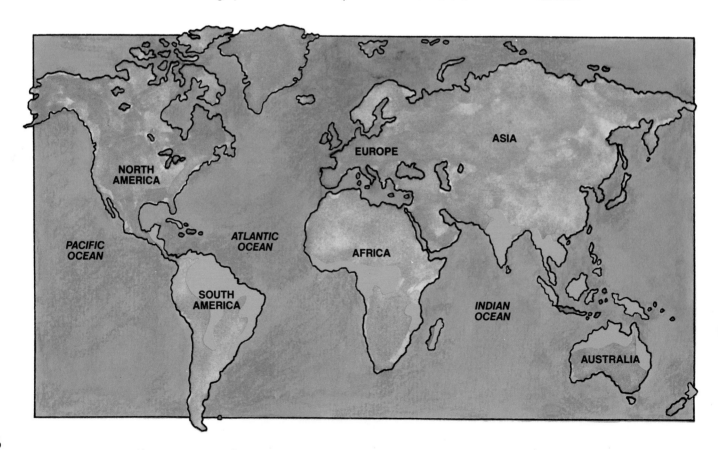

The rainforest floor in Sepilok, Sabah (formerly North Borneo).

to insects, small birds and rodents. The highlands of New Guinea were isolated from the modern world by soaring mountains and dense forests until the 1930s. The islanders there had no wheels available for transport until that time.

As recently as 1971 explorers discovered a "lost" civilization in the Philippine rainforest. These were the Tasaday, who live on the island of Mindanao. They are a gentle, peace-loving people. They have no metal tools and no weapons. The Philippine government wants to preserve the Tasaday culture and protect the people from progress that may destroy their way of life. Many scholars, however, now feel that the "discovery" of the Tasaday may be a hoax.

Two cultures largely untouched by today's world. Left. An Indonesian Dani man with a stone ax. His body is covered with a mixture of pig's fat and charcoal to protect him against the cold night. Right. A Tasaday makes tools in a stream bed. The Tasaday fish for crabs, frogs, tadpoles and small fish in the streams near their caves. These foods provide fundamental protein.

THE AMAZON

The South American rainforest is one of the world's last remote places. Brazil extends over nearly half of South America, and rainforest covers about one-third of Brazil. It is a land of dense jungle, rugged mountains, endless grasslands and mighty rivers, all of which kept foreigners from penetrating into the country's interior until well into the twentieth century.

The Amazon River rises in the Andes Mountains. It has more than a thousand tributaries, and seventeen of them are major rivers over 1,600 km (1,000 mi) long. The basins of the Amazon and Orinoco rivers hold the most extensive rainforests on Earth. The area receives up to 250 cm (100 in) of rain each year. The average temperature is above 25°C (77°F), and between the frequent heavy rainstorms there is almost constant sunshine. But the trees and creepers are so dense that they blot out the Sun. This forest canopy is home to many kinds of mammals, birds and insects. The canopy is formed by the thick branches of trees up to 50m (160 ft) tall, vines and exotic plants such as orchids that grow high in the air.

The American surgeon Hamilton Rice was the first twentieth-century explorer to turn his attention to South America. In 1907 he began a systematic investigation of the Amazon's tributaries. He attempted to reach the Orinoco's source, but fierce tribesmen kept explorers out until a trans-Venezuelan team finally succeeded in 1951, almost fifty years later. In 1925, Rice was one of the first explorers to introduce wireless communication and seaplanes to South American exploration.

The Mato Grosso (Portuguese for "thick forest") Plateau is near the heart of Brazil. Its five major rivers form the Xingu, which meanders 1,600 km (1,000 mi) before flowing into the Amazon near the northeast coast. Situated in the heart of South America, it is home to Indians who resist intrusion.

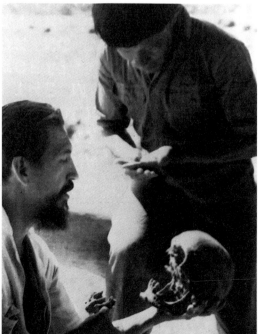

Far left. **Percy Fawcett disappeared without a trace in 1925 while searching for a lost civilization in the Mato Grosso** (above). Left. **Search parties in 1928 and 1933 found only a few belongings from the expedition. Brazilian explorer Orlando Vilasboas holds a skull believed to be that of the ill-fated explorer.**

Writer Jeff Harmon and Indian friends prepare dinner in the Amazon rainforest. Grilled monkey meat is a favorite delicacy.

In 1914 the Rondon-Roosevelt expedition set out to penetrate the Mato Grosso by canoeing 2,400 km (1,500 mi) down the so-called River of Doubt. The river is now renamed Rio Teodoro, after former president Theodore Roosevelt, who led the expedition. Indians attacked the party with poisoned darts. They were drenched by torrential rains. And swarms of aggressive ants and horseflies ravaged the party and its supplies.

Percy Fawcett, an English surveyor, first came to South America in 1906 to explore the borderlands between Bolivia and Brazil. But in 1925 he became obsessed with the idea that the Mato Grosso held the relics of an incredible lost civilization. Fawcett, his son Jack and Raleigh Rimell, one of the younger Fawcett's friends, set out from the city of Cuiaba, near the southern edge of the Mato Grosso. They intended to comb the forest for evidence of a lost city. But the party of three perished in the attempt, probably at the hands of hostile Indians.

The Amazon is a region where superstition still reigns and where tribal doctors preserve an incredible wealth of plant lore. Scientists are eager to preserve these secrets before they are lost. South American plants yield some of the most effective drugs known to medical science. Curare, a strong poison used by the natives for hunting and by Western doctors, is made from the resins of a special plant.

A Panare Indian clears land for agriculture. Such slash-and-burn methods are rapidly destroying the rainforest. Sequential crop cycles periodically require new lands: manioc, plantains, sweet potato and beans soon exhaust the soil's nutrients. There is such a thin layer of impoverished soil that new croplands must frequently be found.

ACROSS AFRICA

The Zaire, formerly the Congo, River is more than 4,160 km (2,600 mi) long. It is the principal river of western Africa, and the Congo rainforest is set in its basin about 1,400 km (900 mi) across.

In 1877, H. M. Stanley was the first European to follow the river from the reed-choked upper reaches of its source in the highlands near Moasampanga to its mouth at Banana, on the Atlantic coast. Stanley first found the dense forest, with its canopy of branches intertwined with vines. The Congo rainforest is an environment almost choked with life, swarming with bees, flies, ants, and other insects. It is an area of oppressive heat and humidity, much like a steam bath. Violent storms often bring trees and branches crashing to the ground.

In 1909 two American scientists, the German-born Herbert Lang (1879–1957) and James Chapin (1890–1964), traveled to the rainforests of the region then known as the Belgian Congo. Lang and Chapin's expedition covered 24,000 km (15,000 mi). They collected more than 25,000 animal skeletons, skins or carcasses, 100,000 insect specimens and thousands of tools and art objects made by hand in the Congo. They also made scores of plaster casts of the faces of the native people of the African rainforest.

The Congo rainforest is home to the pygmy tribes, who live in temporary camps in the midst of the dense forest. Pygmies average less than 1.4 m (4.5 ft) in height. They hunt with spears, and they especially look for elephants. They have developed an extensive knowledge of herbs and other plants. Other groups, including the Bantu, live by fishing and farming in permanent settlements thinly dispersed along the banks of the Zaire and its tributaries.

The rainforest has many bird species. The largest bird of prey in Africa is the crowned eagle, with a wingspan of more than 1.8 m (6 ft). The bird's favorite meal is a young antelope or monkey. Chapin wrote a four-volume study of the birds of the Congo. In 1974–75 a British expedition led by John Blashford-Snell had

A photo taken by Herbert Lang in 1913 of a Congo rainforest native in a headdress made from snail shells. Lang and his party brought back over 10,000 photographs. Lang frequently stayed up all night developing pictures.

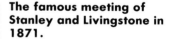

The famous meeting of Stanley and Livingstone in 1871.

Jane Goodall has spent more than three decades observing and studying the primates of Gombe.

many scientific objectives and involved 165 people, including scientists and technicians. They used inflatable boats to negotiate all but seven of the Zaire River's most difficult rapids.

This rainforest is rich in wildlife, and includes monkeys, many kinds of cats, elephants, rhinoceroses and hippopotamuses, antelope, okapi, the giant forest hog and reptiles such as snakes and crocodiles. The habitats of some of these animals extend into the grasslands adjacent to the rainforest.

To the east the dense rainforests of Congo and Zaire give way to patches of more open land. This is the lighter vegetation of the savannas, or grasslands, where monkeys and apes evolved and where the human race may first have appeared. In 1960 a young English scientist, Jane Goodall, set out to live among and study the chimpanzees in the preserve at Gombe near Lake Tanganyika. Since then she has observed more than three generations of chimps and learned much about their habits and social interactions.

John Blashford-Snell is one of the most distinguished of today's explorers in Africa.

A swampy rainforest in Zaire, with raffia palm.

GRASSLANDS

Grasslands, or savannas, are areas where grasses and grains are the predominant types of vegetation. They are found in tropical or subtropical regions near the outer limits of the trade-wind belts. In tropical grasslands the weather is hot or warm all year. During the summer there is a brief rainy period that allows grasses, bushes and low growth to spring up. But the winters are dry, and the vegetation withers. Grasslands may also include trees, especially near rivers, but the predominant vegetation forms are grasses and other low growth. Much of the world's grassland is suitable for grazing or for agriculture.

The most extensive grasslands are in Africa, where they support a variety of grazing cultures. Among the peoples of the African grasslands are the Nuer of the Sudan, the Masai of Tanzania and Kenya and the Karamojong of Uganda. South Africa has a more temperate climate, and its grassland is called *veldt*, from the Dutch word for field. Grasslands spread in a broad band across Africa below the Sahara and alongside the dense rainforests. Nigeria has millions of acres of parklike savanna, with a considerable growth of trees.

The African grassland terrain is usually varied. On the borders of deserts grass is sparse, but on the edge of the tropical rainforests rainfall is higher and trees are more common. These areas are often described as wooded savannas. Baboons, patas and vervet monkeys are often found here. On the Serengeti Plain of East Africa there is abundant wildlife: lions, cheetahs, hyenas, leopards, ostrich, zebras and giraffes. Grasslands are also among the principal areas where zoologists and ethologists (specialists in animal behavior) can study animals and animal behavior.

Grasslands provide a relatively gentle environment for exploration. Permanent camps can be made quite comfortable. They are suitable for sustained research work over periods of years or even decades—a situation that would be difficult or even impossible in the mountains, deserts or rainforests, for example.

Left. **The Masai inhabit the grasslands of Kenya.**

Below. **Dr. Louis Leakey and his wife, Mary, examine a portion of the skull of *Zinjanthropus*. This is an apelike creature they believe to be a distant relative of modern humans.**

The kind of land that "connects" rainforests to the deserts. Left. **Swampy savanna in Zaire.** Right. **The pampas of Argentina.**

There are many grassland sites that are rich in archaeological and anthropological significance (such as at Olduvai Gorge in Tanzania). During the 1960s and 1970s the researcher Richard Leakey and his family spent years in the grasslands of East Africa. Their work was finally rewarded when they located fossilized remains and even footprints from some of the earliest types of apelike creatures. In 1986, Olduvai yielded even more fossil evidence about the early ancestors of modern humans.

In South America the grasslands are known as *llanos* and *campos.* Llanos are the tropical grasslands in the northern part of the continent near the Orinoco River basin. Much of Brazil is covered by the tropical grasslands called campos, which are typical of central and southeastern South America. In Argentina the rugged *pampas* are among the world's best grazing spots for the famed Argentine beef herds. The pampas, named after the Spanish word for "plain," are the temperate grasslands of southern South America farthest from the Equator. Asian grasslands are called *steppes.*

In parts of the world deserts blend almost imperceptibly into the more lush grassland areas where the vegetation is not so sparse and life-forms are more plentiful. Grasslands may expand during times of above-average rainfall and the grasslands that border some of the world's deserts may become parched into desert during prolonged dry periods.

Members of the Nuer tribe of the southern Sudan.

13

DESERTS

Deserts are areas where rainfall is so slight that it cannot support enough vegetation to feed a permanent human population. Deserts may be hot or cold, depending on their latitude, elevation and other factors, but all have deficient rainfall. Hot deserts appear in the hot, dry tropical belts where there is usually high atmospheric pressure. The elevation of the land also affects rainfall. Ironically, rivers that rise in wet regions may pass right through deserts.

In the desert, daytime temperatures are often above 38°C (100°F), and there is less than 25 cm (10 in) of rainfall a year. Sometimes there is just enough water for limited agriculture. Special conservation techniques allow people to raise their crops.

Most of the world's deserts, including the supreme desert, the Sahara, were explored to some extent before the beginning of the twentieth century. The advent of the automobile revolutionized desert travel. The Frenchman André Citroen first motored across the Sahara in 1922. In 1928, L. M. Nesbitt became the first European to cross the Danakil Desert wastelands of eastern Abyssinia (now Ethiopia). Nesbitt lost three of his traveling companions when the Danakil people attacked.

The most famous twentieth-century desert explorer was Wilfred Thesiger. His first desert adventures began in 1930 in the Danakil. In 1933, Thesiger returned to the Danakil country to chart the Awash River. Today most of the Danakil (Afar) people have ceased to be nomads and work on farms. They have become the victims of disease, violence and rapid change.

A modern geologist measures the temperature of a sulfurous spring in the Danakil (Afar) desert of Ethiopia. Below. **The pink areas on the map show the world's deserts.**

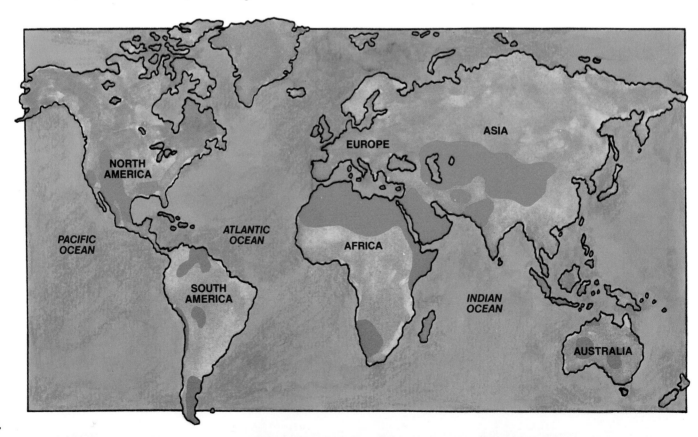

South Africa's Kalahari Desert stretches across approximately 1,500,000 sq km (579,000 sq mi) of Namibia, Angola, Zambia, Zimbabwe, South Africa and Botswana. It is an arid place of scorching heat, and most of the land can be called desert or semidesert. Still it is home to about 50,000 Bushmen of various tribes. The Bushmen make good use of the more than one hundred plants including roots and melons.

The dry air and soil of the desert provide a near perfect environment for preserving the remnants of lost civilizations. Archaeologists estimate that only 40 percent of Egypt's ancient treasures have been recovered. In April 1988 they unearthed three small pyramids that were buried in the sand.

Roughly one-third of Australia is inhospitable desert. Throughout the nineteenth century explorers—including ranchers, government surveyors and prospectors for gold—pieced together an almost complete picture of Australia.

The heat, rough terrain and lack of water made exploring Australia's outback nearly as challenging as the polar regions. One remote portion of Australia, the Simpson Desert, resisted exploration until well into the 1930s. The Simpson Desert covers more than 75,000 sq km (28,958 sq mi) of Australian heartland. Finally, in 1936, the desert was conquered. It took only sixteen days for Edmund Colson and his aboriginal guide, Peter, to cross it. Dr. C. T. Madigan explored the northern portion between 1935 and 1937. In 1967–68, C. Warren Bonython completed a traverse of the desert in thirty-two days.

Left. **Longitudinal dunes giving way to higher desert landforms near Australia's Simpson Desert. Sandstone ridges from 23 to 70 m (70 to 213 ft) rise high from the desert surface.**

Above. **Bushmen archers in South Africa in the 1930s. Even though they tend to be peaceful, the Bushmen sometimes use arrows dipped in slow-acting poison. The Kalahari natives are hunter-gatherers. A hunting and food-gathering way of life is the first step towards a settled agricultural life.**

A modern-day explorer pauses for refreshment at a warm-water spring in the Algerian Sahara.

ASIAN DESERTS

Sven Hedin (1865–1952), a Swedish explorer, made several lengthy expeditions through Central Asia, crossing and crisscrossing the Tibetan plateau. He discovered the ruined cities of the Takla Makan Desert, remnants of an early Mongolian civilization. Between 1886 and 1904, Hedin, Sir Francis Younghusband (1863–1942) and Sir Aurel Stein (1862–1943) explored thousands of miles of little-known territory in Central Asia. Stein and Hedin were among the last of the great scholarly explorers who left impressive writings about their discoveries.

The Gobi Desert spreads across Central Asia east of the Himalayas between the Soviet Union and China. It is essentially rocky. Belts of sand dunes appear in some small scattered areas, but harsh winds have carried away most of the soil and lighter particles. Violent windstorms can whip up clouds of red dust that disguise everything in sight and make it almost impossible to breathe. The Gobi is not as dry as some deserts. It receives about 25 cm (10 in) of rainfall each year.

In 1919 the American Museum of Natural History in New York City sent Roy Chapman Andrews (1884–1960), an American zoologist, to the Gobi. Between 1922 and 1930 he led no less than five expeditions. The Museum of Natural History expected specimens of living flora and fauna.

Andrews's real goal, however, was to find fossilized remains of extinct creatures. To this end he took along a paleontologist, Walter Granger. Paleontology is the scientific study of the fossil remains of past plants and animals. Fossils are frequently found where an arid climate and erosion by wind, rain and river action have exposed the strata of rock.

On July 13, 1923, Andrews discovered a nest of thirteen dinosaur eggs. A few contained shriveled embryos. A mother dinosaur had left them in the nest and covered them with sand 95 million years ago. Not far away were found the remains of Stone Age humans from a much more recent time period.

Left. **Dunes in Outer Mongolia's Gobi Desert.**

Below. **Roy Chapman Andrews counts dinosaur eggs on his third expedition to the Gobi. The dinosaur eggs, discovered in 1922 in the Gobi Desert, were identified as belonging to *Protoceratops*, an ancestor of the horned dinosaurs. The eggs were laid in a spiral in a hollow scooped from the ground.**

In 1928 Granger found the remnants of the 1.5 m (5 ft) long lower jawbone of a mastodon. In 1930 a whole field of mastodon bones including those of an unborn baby mastodon and its mother were found. These dated from a time when lakes, woodlands and bogs covered the area that is now the Gobi Desert.

The Middle East holds some of the least explored terrain on Earth. The Rub' al Khali, or Empty Quarter, is a savage desert within a desert located in southeastern Arabia near the borders of Yemen and Oman. Before World War II, Europeans had visited it only twice in the earlier part of this century. Bertram Thomas made a crossing south to north in 1930–31, and H. St. John Philby had penetrated to its center in 1932. After the war, Wilfred Thesiger made several journeys of exploration and reconnaissance through the Empty Quarter. He first ventured into Arabia's Empty Quarter when O. B. Lean, an entomologist, wanted to study the locust breeding centers in the region. Thesiger then made the desert his life. From his youth he had a burning desire to travel among and to understand the Bedouins.

In recent decades important resources have been discovered in the deserts: oil, natural gas and even vast underground reservoirs of fresh water under the Sahara. These have attracted troops of scientists, engineers and technicians.

Left. **Members of an archaeological expedition excavate the ancient city of Ebla near Tell Mardik in Syria. Because of the arid climate, the desert is a near perfect environment for preserving archaeological finds.**

Above. **Paleontologist Walter Granger with his wife, Anna, on expedition.**

Thesiger's Arabian camels—the great ships of the desert—were used to the rigorous conditions of the desert and helped him survive many dangerous situations.

MOUNTAINS

The sport of mountain climbing was born in 1798, when the Swiss-born scientist de Saussure offered a prize to anyone who could scale Mont Blanc, Europe's highest peak. Mont Blanc rises 4,800 m (15,748 ft) and straddles the borders of Switzerland, France and Italy. De Saussure's observations of mountain rocks laid the foundations of modern geology.

Since then, the Alps have been the proving ground for European climbers. Some mountains are more difficult to climb, not because of their heights but because of their steepness and the difficulty of finding a handhold or foothold on their surfaces. The summit of one of the challenging Alpine peaks, the Eiger, was reached in 1858. But its mile-high north face, the steepest in the Alps, was not conquered until 1938. Chunks of rock and ice frequently break away. Only the bravest and most experienced climbers try it.

Mountain climbers face many dangers. There is always the danger of an avalanche, when great shelves of snow and ice come crashing down. Mountaineers depend upon weather conditions for the success of their expeditions. They may sit for days at the foot of a mountain waiting for a good forecast.

Mountains have their own microclimates—frigid temperatures, winds that may blast more than 160 kph (100 mph), and the prospect of sudden storms. Despite the snow and ice, the heat of the midday sun can be searing. Goggles protect the eyes against glare and ultraviolet rays, and oil or pomade must be used to shield the skin from the sun and wind.

The gray areas show the world's mountains.

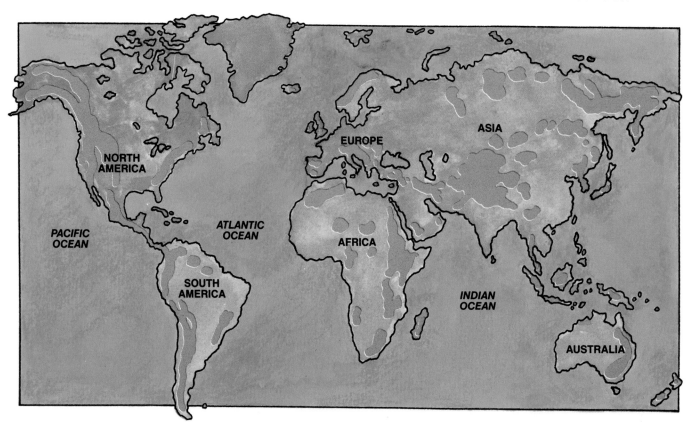

The Alps were the first mountains to be explored. Peaks such as the Eiger still present formidable challenges.

There are two basic approaches to tackling a mountain peak. Climbers who carry all their supplies with them use the Alpine method. In the "siege" or "camp series" method, groups of porters ferry supplies between camps as one team or another pushes slowly toward the summit. This method has been used to conquer Asia's great peaks. Sometimes aircraft drop off food and supplies. For either method, the climbers are usually broken up into smaller teams; only a few of these people will actually try to reach the mountaintop. Water has to be melted from snow and ice, but fuel is at a premium, since most of it must be carried up the mountainside. Sometimes it is necessary to hack out an ice cave or to make a level platform to set up a tent to spend the night.

Reinhold Messner has conquered all fourteen of the Himalayas' peaks, which are almost 8,000 m (24,384 ft) high, without oxygen. Above this height air becomes too thin for most people to live more than a few hours. Messner began by climbing the Himalayan Nanga Parbat (8,745 m; 26,657 ft). He climbed Lhotse in October of 1986. In Europe he has become famous as a guest on talk shows and as the author of numerous magazine stories and books.

Reinhold Messner "warms up" his mountain-climbing skills on nylon ropes suspended from the roof of his Alpine chalet. He climbs with a minimum of equipment: a tent, a change of clothes and an extra pair of climbing boots. He has most frequently worked without guides and base camps for support. His achievements have ushered in a whole new era in mountain climbing.

A mountain climber scales a glacier on Europe's Mont Blanc.

THE ROOF OF THE WORLD

Asia is the undisputed leader among the continents for having the highest mountain peaks. Most of these are clustered in or near the Himalayas, a chain of mountains 2,880 km (1,740 mi) long, with fourteen peaks over 7,900 m (24,070 ft) and more than two hundred peaks over 7,000 m (21,330 ft). The kingdom of Nepal stretches for about 640 km (400 mi) along a ridge of the Himalayas and contains eight of the world's fourteen highest mountains. The Himalayas are still growing, at approximately 5 cm (2 in) every ten years.

In 1936, Bill Tilman of Great Britain ascended the Nanda Devi, at 7,816 m (25,600 ft), the highest and most difficult peak in the Himalayas climbed to that date. In 1950 the French Alpine Club organized the successful Annapurna expedition and selected Maurice Herzog to lead a team of climbers. These climbers had perfected their skills in the Alps.

Herzog's 1950 French expedition to Annapurna conquered the first of the 8,000 m (24,384 ft) peaks. The climbing season in the Himalayas is short. It extends from the end of winter in late March to the end of May or June, when monsoons bring inclement weather. Herzog's expedition was plagued by disaster almost every step of the way. After reaching the top, Herzog accidentally dropped his climbing gloves and watched in horror as they slid down the mountainside. He suffered severe frostbite, and several fingers had to be amputated from his swollen hands.

One by one the Himalayan giants were conquered. Mount Everest, the queen of all mountains, was the major achievement of twentieth-century mountaineering. It is 9,523m (29,028 ft) high. The mountain was named after Sir George Everest, who first mapped and measured the mountain in 1852. Its Tibetan name, "Chomolungma," means "the Goddess Mother of the World."

The first serious British assault on Everest was directed by George Leigh-Mallory in 1921. This expedition stopped at 7,000 m (21,336 ft), hampered by exhaustion brought on by strenuous efforts. Stories told by Tibetans of the monster known as the Abominable Snowman were first circulated by returning members of this expedition. Perhaps susceptible imaginations were deceived when witnesses claimed to have observed some type of animal in the rarefied atmosphere! In 1951, Eric Shipton brought back photographs of tracks in the snow, some 30 cm (12 in) long, but experts believe they were made by a bearlike animal and were enlarged by sunlight melting the snow.

In 1924, on yet another attempt, Leigh-Mallory and A. C. Irvine, a student from England's Oxford University, were last seen climbing at a height of 8,604 m (26,225 ft). After a snow cloud enveloped them, they were never seen or heard of again, and their remains have never been found.

Two famous shots of Tenzing (above) **and Tenzing with Sir Edmund Hillary** (below) **about to reach the summit of Mount Everest in 1953.**

On June 2, 1953, Queen Elizabeth II ascended the throne of England. At the same time, news of the British Everest expedition's successful ascent of the giant mountain almost stole the headlines from the new queen. The Everest expedition was organized and led by Col. H.J.C. Hunt. It included fourteen experienced European mountaineers and was supported by thirty-six porters, or sherpas. The porters were there to carry the 4,530 kg (10,000 lb) of baggage, cameras and supplies.

The 1953 British Expedition basically followed the same route as earlier climbers had tried. But with improved oxygen supplies and more seasoned climbers, their bid was successful. During the climb Edmund Hillary and Tenzing Norkay distinguished themselves as the pair with the most promise of pressing toward the top.

Their final ascent began at 4:00 A.M. on May 29, 1953, in perfect weather, with just a slight breeze. By 6:30 the pair had breakfasted on meltwater and had assembled their gear, strapped on their heavy oxygen packs and struggled into their frozen boots. By 9:00 A.M. they had reached the south summit, and by 11:30 they had reached the main summit. From beginning to end, the whole expedition lasted eighty days.

Left. **Members of the ill-fated 1924 Mallory expedition. Mallory is second from left in the back row.**

Above. **K2 in Pakistan. As recently as 1987 there were claims, based on electromagnetic satellite data, that this mountain peak could be higher than Mount Everest by 30 m (104 ft).**

Nepalese sherpas on an Everest trek. For centuries the porters have rubbed yak butter on their skin and hair to protect it. To date, the summit of Everest has been reached by seven women and about a hundred men in a number of separate expeditions.

NEW WORLD MOUNTAINS

Mountain climbing in the New World began in the sixteenth century when Spanish conquistadors scaled Mexico's Popocatepetl in search of sulfur to fire their guns and cannons. They found it in the volcano's craters, but they also found snow and icy temperatures that they weren't prepared for. Many of them suffered frostbite.

The New World's highest mountain peaks are the Andes Mountains of South America. Unlike Asian peaks, the highest New World mountains are of volcanic origin. But even the tallest are more than a mile shorter than the highest Asian summits. They are all part of the great *cordillera*, or mountain chain, that runs along the Pacific from Alaska down through Central America and the Andes to Chile. Even Antarctica's great peak, the Vinson Massif, in the Sentinel Range, is part of the same chain.

The largest peak outside Asia is Mount Aconcagua, which straddles the border of Chile and Argentina. It is 6,960 m (21,214 ft) high. In 1897 the English mountaineer Edward A. Fitzgerald led an expedition to the top.

The Andes revealed one of their greatest secrets in 1911 when the American explorer Hiram Bingham discovered the ruins of Machu Picchu. This mountaintop city was once a stronghold of the Inca Empire. It had remained hidden for four centuries and was never found and destroyed by the Spanish conquistadors. The citadel of massive ruins clings to the mountainsides and is surrounded by cliffs that plunge 610 m (1,900 ft) into the valleys below. In 1912, Yale University and the National Geographic Society sponsored a joint expedition under Bingham's leadership to investigate the site.

Annie Peck, an American adventurer and explorer who made many expeditions to South American mountain peaks. After a long career in teaching, she took up mountain climbing when she was in her fifties.

The inspiring ruins of Machu Picchu, discovered in the early years of the twentieth century by Hiram Bingham.

Today the high mountains of South America are still home to many Indians, including descendants of the Incas, the Aymara and Quechua. They live in the Altiplano of the Andes, which has an average elevation well over 3.2 km (2 mi). The Indians of the Altiplano are of special interest to scientists who study their medical problems and traditional remedies based on age-old herbal lore. Dandelion juice is used to treat kidney disease, while high blood pressure is treated with parsley.

Mount McKinley in Alaska is North America's highest peak and the most northerly of the world's tallest mountains. In 1913 an American Episcopal priest, Hudson Stuck (1863–1920), led a party of three others to the summit, the first of many expeditions.

Some climbers consider Mount McKinley a bigger challenge than Everest, since reaching the summit requires a vertical climb of 4,000 m (12,192 ft) up the face of Kahiltna Glacier, almost 610 m (1,900 ft) higher than the equivalent segment of Everest. Mount McKinley has claimed the lives of more than fifty climbers.

In February 1984, Naomi Uemura of Japan became the first mountain climber to tackle the 6,193 m (18,876 ft) peak alone in winter. On the way down, however, he was lost in a storm. Four years later an Alaskan climber, Vernon Tejas, made it to the summit. Tejas spent thirty days with a 5 m (16 ft) aluminum ladder strapped to his back to keep him from slipping into crevasses in the surface of the glacier. Before returning, he left a Japanese flag there in honor of Uemura.

Left. **A distance of two miles separates the two distinct peaks of Mount McKinley.** Below. **Mountaineers climb Cotopaxi, a volcano in Ecuador.**

ISLANDS

Islands are land masses surrounded on all sides by water. Some islands were once parts of continents and were formed when sea levels changed. Other islands have been "born" from time to time as a result of volcanic activity on the ocean floor.

Isolation over long periods of time—in many cases, thousands or even millions of years—has led to the development of lifeforms unlike those found in other parts of the world. Similarly, languages and cultures developed by island peoples tend to be distinctive and show greater contrasts than are found, for example, among mainland cultures.

The Galápagos Islands are a Pacific island chain of volcanic origin located near the Equator. Scientists think the islands emerged from the sea some 10 million years ago. The thirteen large and many smaller islands are located about 1,045 km (650 mi) west of Ecuador. The islands have been known since 1535, when a Spanish explorer named them for the giant land tortoises found there. In 1835, the naturalist Charles Darwin visited the islands and collected scientific data that helped him formulate his theories.

The Galápagos are home to many unusual lifeforms in addition to the tortoises. There are several species of land and sea iguanas and unique bird life, including a flightless cormorant. When visitors first came to the islands, they found the animals surprisingly tame because of their long isolation free from predators.

Since 1967 the Galápagos Islands have been the site of a satellite tracking station convenient for scanning both Southern and Northern hemispheres. Twentieth-century naturalists continue to study the rare species and their independent evolution in this living laboratory.

Easter Island is a small island in the South Pacific. It consists of 119 sq km (46 sq mi) of grasslands and outcroppings of rock. It is 3,540 km (2,200 mi) west of Chile, off the coast of South America.

Ring-tailed lemurs are native only to Madagascar. There are between twenty and twenty-seven species of lemurs. Over 95 percent of Madagascar's animal species are unique to the island.

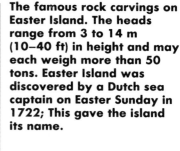

The famous rock carvings on Easter Island. The heads range from 3 to 14 m (10–40 ft) in height and may each weigh more than 50 tons. Easter Island was discovered by a Dutch sea captain on Easter Sunday in 1722; This gave the island its name.

The eruption and "discovery" of Surtsey. Surtsey emerged above the Mid-Atlantic ridge, part of the great chain of volcanic activity that circles the globe.

Among the island's most interesting features are hieroglyphic writings and monolithic stone heads carved from the native *tufa*, a soft volcanic rock. The sculptures are of unknown origin, and may be hundreds or even thousands of years old. Various researchers have tried to link the heads to Scandinavian, Egyptian, Hindu, Oriental or early Andean civilizations. Or they may simply be the work of the early Polynesians—ancestors of the people who live there now.

Madagascar is 2½ times the size of Great Britain and the fourth largest island in the world. It lies off the southeast coast of Africa. Zoologists go to Madagascar to study the many forms of wildlife there. Madagascar separated from the African mainland about 100 million years ago, and here plants and animals have followed an independent path of evolutionary development. The island has a varied terrain. A small desert area has thorny, leafless plants similar to cactuses. There is a strip of rainforest along Madagascar's eastern coast that is watered by heavy rains from the Indian Ocean.

Two creatures that are found only on the Galápagos Islands off the coast of Ecuador. Above. **A blue-footed booby.** Below. **A land iguana,** another of the Galápagos's unique species.

In 1963 a new island "discovered itself" 32 km (20 mi) off the coast of Iceland. In just twenty-four hours a new island was born. It was named Surtsey, after a figure of Icelandic folklore. The birth began with an undersea explosion that sent clouds of smoke, steam and ash billowing above the sea. A black cone of volcanic rock soon appeared above the waves surrounded by dozens of vents spewing streams of red-hot lava. Today the island covers more than 5.2 sq km (2 sq mi). Many kinds of plants, insects and birds have already made the island their home. Other animals—and even people—may live there soon.

Less than ten years later, on January 23, 1973, another spectacular Icelandic eruption added nearly a square mile of new land to the island of Heimaey. Surtsey and Heimaey both stand on top of an undersea ridge of volcanic activity that girdles the globe.

Halfway around the world from Iceland, 27 km (17 mi) south of the island of Hawaii and 914 m (3,000 ft) beneath the Pacific Ocean, a new island waits to be born. Louite is the island's name, but its birth is a long way off. It may take another 10,000 years before the island can be seen above the surface of the ocean.

CAVES

The underground world of caves can give scientists important clues about the geologic past. Caves are usually formed when ground water wears away soft layers of rock. Delicate mineral formations—stalactites and stalagmites—and mineral columns are created by the incessant drip of mineral-laden water. Caves the world over maintain a constant 6–10° C (44–50° F) temperature range. They are found only in the upper portion of the Earth's crust. At depths of more than 1 km (.6 mi), the Earth's temperature and pressure are so great that rock flows or is compressed to fill any hollow or cavity.

Archaeologists were among the first explorers to venture underground. Caves were among mankind's earliest shelters, and the many fossils, tools and paintings that have been found in caves provide insight into human development. Many deep caves have been found in the Pyrenees, the mountains that separate France from Spain. France's Dordogne River Valley is sometimes called the cradle of prehistory, since so many caves and other sites connected with Stone Age human culture have been found there.

In the nineteenth century an Austrian named Antonio Lindner explored a cave near Trieste, Italy, to a depth of 329 m (1,000 ft). This remained the record for deep caving until the twentieth century. In the 1920s and 1930s, cave explorers first used diving equipment for going through perpetually water-filled passages called sumps, or siphons. A siphon is a segment of cave completely filled with water from floor to ceiling. Water-filled cave passages are a particular hazard for cave explorers. Rainfall can cause underground streams to fill tunnels rapidly. After World War II improved diving equipment made rapid advances in cave diving possible. Wet suits protect cave divers from hypothermia—the dangerous state of becoming super-chilled.

Most caves or caverns are formed by the ceaseless flow of underground water gradually wearing away relatively soft layers of porous rock.

The "Big Room" of New Mexico's Carlsbad Caverns, one of the world's most famous caves.

26

Siphons can range in size from a few feet to several thousand feet in length, and they may be separated by dry, air-filled passages. Cavers must dive through siphons using air tanks.

At 232 km (140 mi) long, Mammoth Cave in Kentucky is the largest known cave on Earth. Carlsbad Caverns in New Mexico may be more extensive and many passages remain to be explored. Today zoologists study the huge bat colonies there. Scotland's Holloch Cave is about 130 km (80 mi) long.

Scientists now think the caves of Mexico's largely unexplored Huautla Plateau may be the world's deepest cave system. Winding tunnels, shafts that plunge vertically for hundreds of feet and chains of submerged tunnels linked by raging torrents and roaring waterfalls have kept explorers away.

In 1988 scientists announced the "discovery" in Arizona of a major new cave system. The cave's location was kept quiet for several years until security arrangements could be made. Its passages are approximately 4,000 m (13,000 ft) long and range in height from 15 to 30 m (50-100 ft).

Water-filled caves support life forms from wholly new classes of organisms. Such creatures have followed separate but parallel paths of development for more than 100 million years. Some caves are like ancient seas where tiny organisms survive from primitive times.

Scientists kept a secret for almost fourteen years, until they announced in 1988 that this large cave in Arizona would become a national park.

Recyclable oxygen tanks will one day allow divers to plumb the vast extent of underwater caves. The United States maintains a deep caving team to explore caves like this one.

A SHRINKING WORLD

"Remote" is a relative term, depending on where you live. You may live in a great urban center like New York or London or Los Angeles. Or you may live somewhere like the Andes or in the rainforests of New Guinea. Places are remote because they are far away or hard to reach. A cavern may pass close to or even underneath a great city, but if no one knows about it, it is still remote. But few unknown places remain.

In South America, each year an area of rainforest about half the size of California is cleared. Scientists are working against the clock to describe and document species before they disappear forever along with their habitats. They are exploring ways to prevent the demise of the forests and of the unique species they contain. Some scientists predict that in 50 to 100 years there will be no rainforests left, the victims of civilization's advance.

The loss of huge tracts of rainforest may change the Earth's climate. In 1987, several Western nations, under the leadership of the U.S. space agency (NASA), and in cooperation with various South American governments, conducted a massive expedition to learn more about rainforests and how they affect world climate. The deforestation of Central American forests is already affecting the water level in the Panama Canal and the amount of carbon dioxide in the air.

Drought and deforestation are helping the desert advance. In the Sahel, an area of marginal grassland south of the Sahara, overgrazing by cattle and goats has destroyed the vegetation. A once-green land is now an arid waste. Because there are no trees and greenery to protect the soil, it dries up and blows away. Most deserts are expanding, gradually eating up needed croplands.

Human efforts can help slow the desert's advance. Dams and irrigation projects, such as those in the western United States, can turn desert into cropland. But irrigation schemes may require up to 3 m (10 ft) of water per acre per year and are thus extremely costly.

Photo of the Amazon River basin taken from the American satellite Skylab. Photos of desert landforms, also taken from space, have been of tremendous value in showing areas of encroaching desert. Today's desert researchers compare satellite data from Mars with land-based observations.

As wilderness disappears, so do the unique cultures that grew up in such areas. The people become victims of disease, violence and rapid change. It took only a hundred years for European diseases to wipe out the entire native population of Tasmania after Captain Cook first landed there in 1777.

Human cultures are not the only populations that are threatened. Animals face the threat of extinction due to poaching and loss of habitat. The rapidly expanding populations in South America and Africa below the Sahara pose a very real threat to many of the unique animal species that live there. The day may come when the last South American jaguar and the African rhinoceros, to name two, may die out. They will have become as extinct as the dinosaur or the saber-toothed tiger. Scientists and concerned individuals are working to prevent this.

Gone are the days when explorers set out to discover unknown lands or new continents. The trend today is towards smaller, shorter expeditions with clearly defined agendas. Earning immortality by being "first" is no longer an issue. Today's explorers generally know just what they are looking for. The world still has places that have been, and continue to be, the focal point of exploration. But Earth's remote places are becoming fewer.

Two recent photos show that the rainforests are disappearing at an alarming rate. Left. **In Nigeria a road built through a forest has caused a great stand of trees to be destroyed.** Above. **The result of deforestation due to agricultural needs in northern Brazil. Scientists estimate that as many as 21.5 hectares (53 acres) of the world's rainforests are cleared every minute.**

A growing problem: In Namibia, the desert slowly moves in on semiarid land, causing further drought and famine.

DATELINES

1798 Swiss scientist Horace-Benedict de Saussure offers a prize to anyone who can scale Mont Blanc, Europe's tallest Alp.

1877 H.M. Stanley follows the Congo (now Zaire) River to its source.

1895 Sven Hedin begins to cross the western end of the Gobi Desert.

1906–1908 Aurel Stein finds the Caves of the Thousand Buddhas.

1907 Hamilton Rice begins his exploration of the Amazon and its tributaries.

1909 Lang and Chapin begin their expedition of what was then known as the Belgian Congo.

1911 Hiram Bingham uncovers the long-lost ruins of Machu Picchu.

1914 The Rondon-Roosevelt Expedition (headed by U.S. President Theodore Roosevelt) explores the Mato Grosso.

1919 Roy Chapman Andrews begins his journeys to the Gobi Desert.

1921 George Leigh-Mallory mounts the first serious expedition to climb Mount Everest.

1922 The French automobile manufacturer André Citroen motors across the Sahara.

1923 Roy Chapman Andrews discovers a nest of dinosaur eggs.

1925 Percy Fawcett's party is lost in the Amazon.

1928 L. M. Nesbitt becomes the first European to cross Ethiopia's Danakil Desert.

1930 Wilfred Thesiger begins his lifelong career in desert exploration.

1936 Australia's hostile Simpson Desert is crossed by Edmund Colson.

1936 Britain's Bill Tilman climbs Nanda Devi, at that time the highest peak climbed.

1945–50 Wilfred Thesiger makes several journeys through Arabia's Rub' al Khali, the Empty Quarter.

1950 A French team, headed by Maurice Herzog, scales Annapurna, in the Himalayas.

1951 Eric Shipton's photographs taken in the Himalayas suggest evidence that an "Abominable Snowman" might exist.

1953 On May 29 the final ascent, headed by Edmund Hillary and Tenzing Norkay, begins to conquer Mount Everest.

1960 Jane Goodall begins her study of primates on the eastern shore of Lake Tanganyika.

1963 The volcanic island of Surtsey, off the coast of Iceland, "discovers" itself.

1974–75 John Blashford-Snell leads an expedition on the Zaire River.

1984 Naomi Uemura of Japan becomes the first person to tackle Mount McKinley alone in the dead of winter—and doesn't make it.

1984 Mexico's Huautla cave system is explored.

1986 Reinhold Messner climbs the Himalayan Nanga Parbat.

1988 Caves in Arizona that are over 4 km (2½ mi) long are introduced to the public for the first time.

GLOSSARY

ANTHROPOLOGIST A scientist who studies human beings and their origins.

ARCHAEOLOGIST A scientist who studies the remains of past civilizations.

BEDOUIN A nomadic, or wandering, member of a Mideastern or North African desert tribe.

CAMPOS One type of South American grassland.

CANOPY The uppermost leafy layer of a rainforest.

CARNIVOROUS Meat eating.

CORDILLERA A system of mountain ranges.

CURARE A powerful poison used by South Americans for hunting. It has been adapted for positive use in medicine.

DEFORESTATION The cutting down or clearing away of forests.

DESERT Dry land without appreciable water supply.

ECOSYSTEM A pattern of relationships between living things and their environment.

ENTOMOLOGIST A scientist who specializes in the study of insects.

ETHNOLOGIST A scientist who studies human cultures.

ETHOLOGIST A scientist who studies animal behavior.

FOSSIL The remains of a plant or animal that have turned to stone.

GEOLOGIST A scientist who studies the history of the earth.

GRASSLANDS Geographic areas where grasses and grains can be grown successfully.

JUNGLE An Anglo-Indian term (from the word *jangal*) for a dense forest or wilderness.

LINGUIST A person who specializes in the study of languages.

LLANOS Grasslands of South America.

MELTWATER Water that comes from melting snow or ice.

MICROCLIMATE The climate of a small place or habitat.

MONSOON A wind common to the region of the Indian Ocean and southern Asia.

PALEONTOLOGY The study of the past as it is shown by fossil remains.

PAMPAS The grasslands of Argentina.

PRIMATES The order of mammals comprising humans, apes, monkeys and related forms.

RAINFOREST A tropical forest with a heavy annual rainfall.

SAVANNA A tropical or subtropical grassland with scattered trees.

SHERPA A Tibetan living in the area of the Himalayas, usually skilled in mountain climbing.

SIPHON A water-filled cave passage.

STALACTITE A mineral deposit in a cave that hangs down, resembling an icicle.

STALAGMITE A mineral deposit in a cave that appears to be growing upward.

STEPPES Grasslands of Asia.

SUBTROPICAL Relating to an area or areas near the tropical zones.

SUMMIT The highest point, or peak, of a mountain.

TERRAIN The land formation of a geographic area.

VELDT Grasslands of South Africa

INDEX